CHICAGO

MICHAEL E. GOODMAN

THE HISTORY OF THE
CUBS

CREATIVE EDUCATION

Published by Creative Education
123 South Broad Street, Mankato, Minnesota 56001
Creative Education is an imprint of The Creative Company

Designed by Rita Marshall
Editorial assistance by Rosemary Wallner & John Nichols

Photos by: Allsport Photography, Focus on Sports, SportsChrome,
Associated Press/Wide World Photos, Corbis-Bettmann.

Library of Congress Cataloging-in-Publication Data

Goodman, Michael E.
The History of the Chicago Cubs / by Michael E. Goodman.
p. cm. — (Baseball)
Summary: A team history of the Chicago Cubs, featuring outstanding
players over the years.
ISBN: 0-88682-903-8

1. Chicago Cubs (Baseball team)—History—Juvenile literature.
[1. Chicago Cubs (Baseball team)—History.   2. Baseball—History.]
I. Title.   II. Series: Baseball (Mankato, Minn.)

GV875.C6G665   1999
796.357'64'0977311—dc21   97-1873

First edition

9 8 7 6 5 4 3 2 1

The ever-present breeze that whips and whirls through the streets of Chicago fits the Midwestern metropolis's famous nickname—the "Windy City." The same strong currents that buffet the shores of nearby Lake Michigan also find their way to another Chicago landmark, Wrigley Field. The ivy-covered walls of the North Side ballpark have provided a home for baseball's Chicago Cubs since the 1920s, and many of the game's great moments have occurred within these "friendly confines."

While Wrigley Field is one of the smallest-capacity stadiums in the major leagues, it is one of the largest in terms of

Chicago superstar Billy Williams.

the noise generated by the faithful Cubs followers. The ballclub and its fans share a special relationship. This love affair goes back to 1876, when the team first joined the National League, and it has continued on through 10 National League championships and two World Series titles.

Players like Hack Wilson, Gabby Hartnett, Ernie Banks, Billy Williams, Ryne Sandberg, and recently Sammy Sosa have all taken their turn providing thrills, and Chicago's fans have been there every step of the way.

From the very start, the Cubs founders appreciated the fans as much as they did their players. That appreciation helped get the National League—and modern day baseball—under way.

1 8 7 6

William A. Hulbert became president of the new NL, a position he held until his death six years later.

1876: A NEW LEAGUE IS FOUNDED

The Cubs' founding father was William A. Hulbert, who owned the team in the 1870s, then called the White Stockings. In 1875, Hulbert found himself faced with a dilemma. Like several other teams, the White Stockings were piling up losses on the field, and off of it. Problems such as poor playing and gambling scandals were threatening to destroy professional baseball.

Hulbert decided to take action. He met with owners of the most successful clubs in the old National Association to convince them to form a new league. The organization—to be called the National League—would have strict rules concerning the behavior of players.

Before Chicago played its first game in the new league, Hulbert made sure his team included some of baseball's top

Steve Trachsel, a key man in the Cubs' rotation.

talent. He convinced several outstanding players to come to Chicago, including pitcher/manager Albert Spalding.

With Spalding's help, the White Stockings got off to a great start in the new league. In the team's very first game, Spalding fired a 4–0 shutout to beat Louisville, one of an astounding 47 wins the iron-armed pitcher had that year. Chicago went on to win the first-ever National League pennant with a record of 52–14.

A few years later, Spalding left his playing days behind to set up a sporting goods company, which still exists today. He also took over as president of the Chicago club and hired a new player/manager named Adrian "Cap" Anson, who led the team to five pennants between 1880 and 1886, and who, in 1939, became only the second Cubs player to be inducted into baseball's Hall of Fame (after Grover Cleveland Alexander in 1938).

"Cap Anson was a baseball pioneer," said one writer. "He was one of the first to use coaching signals, the hit-and-run, a pitching rotation, and spring training. He was also a mean-spirited guy who marched his team onto the field in military formation and demanded very strict behavior. His players often hated him, but he helped them become winners."

On August 6, player/manager Cap Anson slammed three homers in three consecutive at-bats.

TURN-OF-THE-CENTURY CUBS BUILD LEGACY

Al Spalding and Cap Anson helped the White Stockings become a National League power in the late 1800s, but by 1906 a new manager named Frank Chance had taken over the team.

The ballclub was at that time known as the Cubs to some

fans, but to others the Colts, the Nationals, and even the Spuds. It was a common practice for teams in the late 19th and early 20th centuries to go by several nicknames at one time. It wouldn't be until 1907 that the team would finally settle on Cubs as their official nickname.

In Chance's first season as manager, the 1906 club set a mark for excellence that may never be bettered. Boasting two outstanding pitchers in Ed Reulbach and Mordecai "Three Fingers" Brown, who had lost part of his right index finger and paralyzed his little finger in a childhood farm accident, the team won an amazing 116 games while losing only 36. Between 1906 and 1908, the two hurlers were near perfection. They compiled a record of 135 wins and only 36 losses, leading the Cubs to three straight National League pennants.

1 9 1 0

Cubs pitcher Mordecai "Three Fingers" Brown led the club in strikeouts with 143.

In the 1906 World Series, however, the heavily favored Cubs were upset by their crosstown rivals the Chicago White Sox in six games. White Sox ace pitcher Ed Walsh baffled the Cubs' powerful lineup with his then-legal spitball, winning two games in the series while striking out 17. "I swear the ball disintegrated on the way to the plate," said one frustrated Cub. "All I saw was the spit going by."

The next year was very different. The Cubs broke through and won their first World Series title by sweeping the Detroit Tigers in four straight games.

In 1908 the Cubs would best Ty Cobb and the Tigers again to claim their second straight championship. But if it weren't for a quick-thinking play made in September, there might not have been a World Series victory that year for the Cubs to celebrate.

The New York Giants and the Cubs were locked in a race

Former Cubs reliever Mitch Williams.

1989 Rookie of the Year Jerome Walton.   11

*Gabby Hartnett
began a Cubs
career that
spanned 18 years—
three of them as
a manager.*

and were playing a crucial series in New York during the last days of the season. The Cubs had won the first two games and the third was tied in the bottom of the ninth. Two Giants runners were on base—Moose McCormick on third and Fred Merkle on first. The player at bat smashed a single to center field. Giants fans began to pour onto the diamond as McCormick crossed the plate. Merkle, seeing the crowd and not wanting to get trampled, decided to head for the locker room without touching second base. To complete the play, Merkle had to step on second or he could be forced out, and the run wouldn't count.

"Everyone thought the game was over," recalled Giants player Fred Snodgrass. "Everyone except Johnny Evers, anyway." The Cubs' second baseman had noticed Merkle had not touched second and began to yell and scream until two teammates chased down a fan who had made off with the ball. Once the ball was retrieved, shortstop Joe Tinker threw the would-be souvenir back to Evers, who jumped up and down on second base until umpire Hank O'Day ruled that Merkle was out and the Giants' run didn't count. Extra innings couldn't be played because of the riotous conditions, so the game was called a tie.

The Cubs and Giants went on to finish the season deadlocked, so a one-game playoff was set up to decide which team advanced to the World Series. In a tense battle, Three Fingers Brown came on in relief to duel Giants great Christy Mathewson, and the Cubs prevailed 4–2. Thanks to Johnny Evers' heads-up play in September, the Cubs played and won a World Series they might not have even been in. Sadly, the team has never captured a World Series since.

The Cubs were up and down over the next 20 years. They topped the National League again in 1910 and 1918 but then began to sink in the standings. They finally hit rock bottom in 1925, finishing eighth in the National League with a disappointing 68–86 record.

Fortunately for the Cubs, help was on its way. In the mid-1920s two new stars arrived in the Windy City to bolster the team. They were "Gabby" Hartnett and "Hack" Wilson.

Charles Leo Hartnett was one of the finest defensive catchers in baseball for 20 seasons and was also an excellent hitter. Hartnett did one other thing very well—he loved to talk to opposing batters and distract them at the plate. Before long, sportswriters began calling him "Gabby," and the nickname stuck.

For the fourth consecutive season slugger Hack Wilson led the National League in homers.

Gabby may have annoyed opponents with his chatter, but his teammates loved him. Charlie Root, who pitched to Hartnett for 16 years in Chicago, said, "He got the best out of you. If you were letting down, Gabby would fire the ball back at you like a shot. Believe me, that woke you up on the mound. He was daring at all times and sure of himself. He made a pitcher feel that way, too."

In 1926 Gabby was joined on the team by Lewis Wilson, a short, powerful slugger. Wilson looked like a famous wrestler of the time, George Hackenschmidt, so teammates began calling him "Hack." Short and stocky, Wilson packed an incredible punch for a man barely 5-foot-6, but what he lacked in height he made up for in brute strength. Wilson carried 200 well-muscled pounds on his short frame and

1 9 5 3

The celebrated career of Ernie Banks, known to fans as "Mr. Cub," began in Chicago.

needed an 18-inch collar for his shirts. With his unorthodox tomahawk swing, he regularly smashed screaming line shots over the fences at Wrigley Field.

In his best season, 1930, Wilson set two amazing records —56 homers, a National League record until 1997; and 190 runs batted in, a total never topped in the National or American League.

Hartnett and Wilson led Chicago back to the top of the National League in 1929, but the team lost the World Series to the Philadelphia Athletics. The Cubs captured pennants in '32 and '35 as well, but still fell short in the World Series.

Chicago was beginning to see a trend: every three years, the Cubs seemed to come out on top. So, as the 1938 season approached, fans figured that if form held true, it would be an exciting year. They were right.

The pennant race came down to the wire with the Pittsburgh Pirates leading the Cubs by a half-game. The two teams faced off in Chicago, and after eight innings the score was tied 5–5. But there was a problem: it was getting dark. There were no lights at Wrigley Field, and the umpires announced that if neither team scored in the ninth, the game would be called.

With that in mind, the Cubs retired the Pirates in order in the top half of the inning, but didn't fare much better to start the bottom. The first two Cubs batters made outs. Then Gabby Hartnett stepped to the plate.

By this time, Hartnett was the Cubs' player/manager and was nearing the end of his playing career. The darkness made it nearly impossible to see, and Hartnett took two quick strikes from Pirates reliever Mark Brown. When the

Andre "Hawk" Dawson's size made him an intimidating hitter.

Legendary Hall-of-Famer Ernie Banks.

next pitch came whizzing toward the plate, Gabby swung where he thought the ball might be, and he connected. The ball sailed toward the left field stands, and while many of the players have said they couldn't even see the ball go over the wall, the fans in left certainly did. A huge roar went up as Gabby Hartnett's famous shot, known as the "the homer in the gloaming [darkness]" helped make the Cubs National League champions once again.

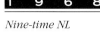

Nine-time NL All-Star third base-man Ron Santo won his fifth Gold Glove award.

LET'S PLAY TWO: ERNIE BANKS

While the Cubs haven't won a World Series since 1908, they came close in 1945, capturing one final National League pennant before steadily declining for the next 20 years. Some great players starred in Chicago during the 1950s and 1960s, but they never got to wear a World Series ring. Among those "ringless" stars were "Iron Man" Billy Williams, who once played in 1,117 consecutive games and was one of baseball's top outfielders; power-hitting third baseman Ron Santo; smooth-fielding shortstop Don Kessinger; and pitching stars Moe Drabowsky, Ken Holtz-man, and Ferguson Jenkins.

But perhaps the Cubs player who most deserved a World Series ring was a slender, power-hitting shortstop named Ernie Banks. Blessed with an enthusiasm that would never wane during his 19 seasons, Banks won the hearts of Cubs fans with his warm smile, big bat, and sure glove. His great love of baseball overrode the fact that, for the majority of his career, the Cubs were a losing team. In a testament to his great spirit, whenever anyone would ask Banks what the

Ryne Sandberg, a well-rounded talent (pages 18-19).

conditions for the game were like, Banks would invariably say—rain or shine—"It's a beautiful day for baseball. Let's play two [a doubleheader]."

Physically, Banks didn't look like a slugger. Though he was 6-foot-1 and weighed only 180 pounds, he had powerful wrists and arms. "You grab hold of him," said Cubs manager Bob Scheffing, "and it's like grabbing hold of steel."

Every year fans could count on Ernie Banks. Five times he slugged 40 or more home runs in a season. No shortstop in history had ever had that kind of power. The Cubs finished in sixth place in two of those years, 1958 and 1959, but sportswriters recognized his unique greatness. They elected him the league's Most Valuable Player both seasons. Banks retired after the 1971 season, finishing with career numbers that stand out on the page: 2,583 hits, 1,636 RBIs, .274 batting average, 11 All-Star Games, a Gold Glove, and 512 home runs.

After Banks retired, the Cubs hoisted a pin-striped pennant with the number 14 atop the left field foul pole at Wrigley Field. He was the first Cubs player ever to have his number retired, and in 1977, Banks was inducted into the Baseball Hall of Fame—fitting tributes to the man Chicago fans lovingly refer to as "Mr. Cub."

Future Hall-of-Famer Ferguson Jenkins returned to Chicago after a nine-year absence.

RYNO AND THE RED BARON RAISE HOPES

Ernie Banks almost got to play on a championship Cubs team in 1969. That year Chicago jumped out to an early lead in the National League East Division and were up by nine and one-half games over the New York Mets in mid-August. Banks, Ron Santo, and Billy Williams each hit more than 20 home runs that season, and Ferguson Jenkins won 21 games. But the Cubs faded in late August, losing eight in a row while the Mets won 10 straight.

Santo, Williams, and Jenkins were still with the club in 1973, when Chicago broke out to another early lead. But once again the Mets caught them. From that point the Cubs faded out of sight.

It would take 11 years for the Cubs to break their string of non-playoff seasons, and for the Chicago faithful, it was a long wait. Led by a 23-year-old second baseman named Ryne Sandberg and a wily veteran pitcher named Rick Sutcliffe, the 1984 Cubs erased the memory of past collapses by bringing home the National League Eastern Division title.

Ryne Sandberg established an NL record for fielding percentage by a second baseman with a .9938 mark.

Cy Young Award winner Greg Maddux.

"The Red Baron," pitcher Rick Sutcliffe.

Sutcliffe, a mid-season acquisition from the Cleveland Indians, had always been known as a pitcher who was at his best when the stakes were high. The cellar-dwelling Indians had a record of 4–5 when they traded Sutcliffe, who thrived in the fiercely contested division race. When the 240-pound, 6-foot-5 hurler went 16–1 for the Cubs, he was rewarded with the National League Cy Young Award.

With his mountainous stature and full red beard, Sutcliffe intimidated many batters before they even got into the box. "Sutcliffe's a good guy, but he's got a mean streak in him," said Cubs catcher Jody Davis. "Batters look out at that big-bearded rascal and they know he's coming inside all day long. Rick can get in your head."

The combination of the red beard, intimidating look, and untouchable pitches earned Sutcliffe the nickname "The Red Baron," which referred to the similarly intimidating World War I German fighter pilot.

The trade for Sutcliffe may have been a key factor in the Cubs' success in 1984, but it was actually a trade two years earlier that set the stage for the team's future. A promising but little-known minor-league third baseman, Ryne Sandberg was thrown into a deal where the Cubs and the Philadelphia Phillies exchanged shortstops, the Phillies getting Ivan DeJesus and the Cubs getting Larry Bowa. The aging Bowa wasn't quite a straight-up trade for the younger DeJesus, so Sandberg was included to even out the deal.

Sandberg started out with the Cubs as a third baseman in 1982, but late that season, manager Jim Frey switched him to second base. The move proved to be a perfect fit, and by 1984 Sandberg's talent was in full bloom. He hit .314, scored

1 9 8 7

On August 13, the Cubs retired Hall-of-Famer Billy Williams's jersey, number 26.

114 runs, bashed 19 home runs, had 84 RBIs, and made 32 steals—efforts that earned him the rank of National League Most Valuable Player.

Shawon Dunston made his first All-Star appearance, going 0-for-2.

Sandberg—nicknamed Ryno—also won the Gold Glove as the best-fielding second baseman in the league, and his complete package of talent awed many longtime baseball observers. Cubs radio and television announcer Harry Caray, the legendary voice of the Cubs, summed it up best. "I've been calling big-league games for 40 years, and I can't remember anybody capturing the imaginations of the fans quite like this kid. He's really something."

Sandberg's heroics and Sutcliffe's energy helped the Cubs win their first title of any kind since 1945. After so many near misses, Cubs fans finally had something to be proud of when the headlines read: Chicago Cubs—1984 National League Eastern Division Champs. There was joy in the Windy City once again.

THE HAWK SOARS AT WRIGLEY

Despite their high hopes, the Cubs' happiness was short-lived. Chicago lost to the San Diego Padres in a tight National League Championship Series three games to two. A Chicago sportswriter noted, "Cubs players and fans alike were crushed, dumbfounded. What had seemed all but theirs—the club's first National League pennant since 1945—suddenly slipped through their grasp." As a result, Cubs management began looking for additional stars.

Their first priority was a power hitter. The perfect choice

was Andre Dawson, who was laboring north of the border in Montreal. Dawson, nicknamed "Hawk," had been starring for 10 seasons with the Montreal Expos, but he was ready to move on. A decade of playing on the hard, artificial surface in Montreal had left the once-swift Dawson with a pair of arthritic knees. He needed to play on natural grass if he was to prolong his career, and hitter-friendly Wrigley Field was his first choice.

Left-hander Randy Myers set the National League record for saves in a season with 53.

Dawson wanted so badly to play for the Cubs in Chicago that in March of 1987 he signed a blank contract and told the Cubs management to fill in whatever dollar amount they thought was fair. The Cubs took Hawk up on his offer and the eight-time All-Star didn't disappoint. In his first year with Chicago, Dawson slammed 49 homers, drove in 137 runs, and was named National League Most Valuable Player. "Everybody thought Hawk couldn't do it over a whole season anymore," laughed Sandberg. "He sure proved a lot of people wrong."

With Dawson's big bat in the cleanup spot, Sandberg wreaking his usual havoc, shortstop Shawon Dunston's consistent defensive contributions, and the soon-to-be-named 1989 Rookie of the Year Jerome Walton, the Cubs raced to the top of the National League East again that year. The club's 93–69 mark vaulted them into the National League Championship Series against the hard-hitting San Francisco Giants. The Cubs battled gamely but were defeated four games to one.

Dawson would continue to prove his critics wrong for two more highly productive seasons in Chicago before moving on

to the Boston Red Sox in 1992. The Hawk smashed 174 home runs in only five seasons in Chicago, good enough to place him ninth in Cubs history at the time of his departure.

1 9 9 5

Pitcher Kevin Foster posted 12 wins in his first full season with the Cubs.

SPARKING THE CUBS IN THE '90S

Although the loss to the Giants in the 1989 National League Championship Series was a bitter disappointment, it also marked the beginning of a new era in Chicago.

In the 1989 five-game series, a new star had emerged: Cubs first baseman Mark Grace. Nearly unstoppable, the left-hander hit Giants' pitching at a .647 clip, collecting 11 hits in 17 at-bats. In addition, he belted a homer and drove in a remarkable eight runs.

While he had hit .314, with 13 homers and 79 RBIs, and won the Rookie of the Year Award in 1988, it was the '89 championship series that earned Grace national attention. "Up to that point I never felt much like a leader on the team," explained Grace. "It was always Ryno's [Sandberg] team or Hawk's [Dawson] team before, but during that series I grew up a lot."

Grace has become one of the premier hitting and fielding first basemen in the game. Although he doesn't hit with the power of Dawson or Sandberg, Grace has the innate ability to hit the ball to all fields. "I've never been a big slugger," smiled the four-time Gold Glove award winner. "But I can be very productive by hitting the ball where it's pitched."

When big hitter Sammy Sosa joined the club in 1992, he and Grace became a pair that could drive homers over the ivy-covered Wrigley Field walls with regularity. A native of the Dominican Republic, Sosa brought extraordinary power to the plate. "Sammy is so strong, he makes hitting homers look easy," said former Cubs teammate Brian McRae.

Sosa crunched 40 homers in 1996 while driving in 100 runs. In his first five seasons with the Cubs, he belted a whopping 142 round-trippers. "Sosa's a classic slugger," remarked San Francisco Giants manager Dusty Baker. "Every time up, he might take one deep."

For Cubs fans, watching Grace and Sosa rise to superstar status was a thrilling experience, but at the same time, the team also sustained a major loss. Ryne Sandberg, the superstar second baseman, decided to call it quits after the 1997 season. He had retired once before, in 1995, but couldn't stay away from the game. After making a comeback in 1996 and playing two more seasons, the Cubs great decided he'd finally played enough. "I've worn this uniform a long time, and I'm proud of all I've accomplished as a Cub," said an emotional Sandberg. "But I wish I could have brought the fans here a World Series."

Doug Glanville hit his first major league homer Sept. 11 off Montreal's Jeff Fassero.

BUILDING UP—AGAIN

While the Cubs have been an exciting team to watch in the '90s, they haven't been a part of postseason play since 1989. Grace and Sosa have continued their assault on National League pitching, but lack of pitching skill on their own team had been the club's downfall. In the '90s, the Cubs pinned their hopes on rookie pitcher Jeremi Gonzalez. The Venezuelan native combined a hard fastball with the savvy of a veteran pitcher. "Jeremi is unshakeable," said

Jeremi Gonzales, a young pitcher with potential.

Award-winning first baseman Mark Grace. 31

Rookie pitcher Kerry Wood tied Roger Clemens's major-league record for strikeouts in a game (20) on May 6.

Cubs manager Jim Riggleman. "For a 22-year-old kid to come in from double-A [minor league] ball and show the poise and ability he has is remarkable." Gonzalez went 11–9 during his rookie campaign in 1997. Another Cubs pitcher emerged early in the 1998 season as a star to watch. Rookie Kerry Wood tied the major league record for strikeouts in a game. He then struck out 13 batters in the following game for a total of 33 strikeouts in two consecutive games–a new major league record.

The Cubs were also counting on veterans Kevin Tapani, Mark Clark, and Kevin Foster to form a strong starting staff. "I think we're going to see a very positive change from our pitching," predicted Riggleman. "We've finally got some good balance on our staff."

On the offensive side, the Cubs felt solid through the heart of the order with Grace and Sosa both in their primes and signed to long-term contracts. The team also had high hopes for hard-hitting rookie third baseman Kevin Orie. We think Kevin will develop into a 20-homer, 90-RBI-type player," noted Cubs general manager Ed Lynch.

For Sosa, Grace, and the new crop of Cubs stars, the path may be difficult, but the goal is clear. With an improved pitching staff including Kerry Wood and the further development of youngsters such as Orie, the Cubs are taking all the right steps toward bringing the Windy City its long-awaited third World Series championship.